W9-CBF-847

Pete the Cat Plays Hide-and-Seek

Text copyright © 2022 by Kimberly and James Dean

Illustrations copyright © 2022 by James Dean

Pete the Cat is a registered trademark of Pete the Cat, LLC.

All rights reserved. Printed in the United States of America.

No part of this book may be used or reproduced in any manner whatsoever without

written permission except in the case of brief quotations embodied in critical articles and reviews.

For information address HarperCollins Children's Books, a division of HarperCollins Publishers,

195 Broadway, New York, NY 10007.

www.harpercollinschildrens.com

Library of Congress Control Number: 2022938168

ISBN 978-0-06-309592-2

The artist used pen and ink with watercolor and acrylic paint on

300lb press paper to create the illustrations for this book.

22 23 24 25 26   PC   10 9 8 7 6 5 4 3 2 1

❖

First Edition

Pete the Cat
Plays Hide-and-Seek

Kimberly & James Dean

HARPER

An Imprint of HarperCollinsPublishers

Pete and the gang love to play hide-and-seek!
And who's the fastest seeker? Cool cat Pete.

Since Pete is IT, he covers both his eyes.
Then he counts to ten as everyone hides.

Pete counts quickly!
1 - 2 - 3 - 4 - 5 - 6 - 7 - 8 - 9 - 10!
Then he opens his eyes and looks for his friends.

"READY OR NOT,

Pete looks everywhere. Pete runs to see. Pete quickly thinks, "Where, oh, where could Gus be?"

He spots Gus hiding behind a tree.

But it is not Gus at all! How can that be?

It's just a mailbox hiding behind the tree.

READY OR NOT!
PETE IS STILL IT.

IT'S ALL GROOVY.
'CAUSE PETE NEVER QUITS.

Pete keeps on looking. Pete runs to see.
Pete quickly thinks, "Where, oh, where
could Alligator be?"

Out of sight! Dynamite!

He spots Alligator on the bus to the right.

But that's not Alligator! Pete wants to fuss.

It's just Bob's surfboard sitting on the bus.

IT'S ALL GROOVY.
'CAUSE PETE NEVER QUITS.

Pete keeps on searching. Pete runs to see.
Pete quickly thinks, "Where, oh, where could
Turtle and Squirrel be?"

No doubt! Far out!

"There's Turtle and Squirrel at the playground," he shouts.

But it isn't Turtle at all. Pete starts to groan.
It turns out to be a polka dot stone.

"Aw, man," Pete says, "this wasn't the plan."
That's not Squirrel. It's just a watering can!

Pete takes one last look. Pete runs to see.
Pete thinks quicker, "Where, oh, where
could Grumpy Toad be?"

Whoa! Too Cool!

He spots Grumpy Toad hiding by the pool!

But that isn't Grumpy Toad. Pete starts to sigh.
Why is Granny's armchair sitting poolside?!

Suddenly Pete stops. Is hide-and-seek really fun?
What if he keeps trying and still can't find anyone?!

This time Pete doesn't rush. He takes a slow, deeeeeep breath in.

Then he opens his eyes and looks around again . . .

There's Grumpy. There's Squirrel.
There's Turtle, Alligator, and Gus!

The whole gang says,

"Yay, Pete! You found all of us!"

See? Things aren't always as they first appear.
If you take a deep breath, things become clear!
Pete is a good seeker. He is happy he took his time.

'Cause Pete's favorite part of
hide-and-seek is when he gets to . . .